all-time great classics

THE HOUND
of
The Baskervilles

(A masterpiece of Arthur Conan Doyle)

MANOJ PUBLICATIONS

Publishers :

MANOJ PUBLICATIONS

761, Main Road, Burari, Delhi-110084 (INDIA)

Mobile : 09999476076, 09868112194
08178823569, 08178854810

E-mail : info@manojpublications.com

For online shopping visit our website :
www.sawanonlinebookstore.com

From the Publisher's Desk

In this age of competition, none has the time to go through long novels which seem to have no endings. Maybe these kinds of novels were written during the time when people led leisurely life. They had plenty of time at their disposal. Reading good literary work on weekend was the main source of entertainment. Now the time has entirely changed. Readers search for short, excellent literary works which are comprised of well-designed illustrations. These illustrations clear their themes at very first glance. As a reader flips through the pages of an illustrated novel, each chapter unfolds in a very easy and interesting style.

Keeping this modern approach in mind, we have brought out this novel in a very novel way. Easy-to-understand language accompanied by life-like illustrations has added four-fold beauty to the novel. At the end of the novel, questions based on each and every chapter have been given to test the mental faculty of the reader.

All these outstanding features incorporated in this novel have made it suitable for young and old alike. Undoubtedly, it is ideal for classrooms, library and personal collection too.

About the Author

Arthur Conan Doyle was born in Edinburgh, Scotland, on May 22, 1859. His grandfather, John Doyle, was a caricaturist whose weekly political cartoons were admired and widely circulated. His father, Charles, also an artist, earned most of his meagre income from his position as architect-clerk in the civil service.

A strict schoolmaster made young Arthur's first two school years patently miserable. From age nine through sixteen he attended the preparatory school of Stonyhurst College, after which he had spent a year at a more lenient school in Austria, where he did little to distinguish himself as a student of German, but had great fun playing tuba in the school band.

Upon his return from Austria, Doyle entered the medical school of the University of Edinburgh, where he would meet Dr. Joseph Bell, a surgeon at the Edinburgh infirmary. Thin, wiry, a brilliant diagnostician, it was Bell upon whom Doyle would later model his famous protagonist, Mr. Sherlock Holmes.

Doyle's medical studies were interrupted twice, once in 1880 when he spent seven months as ship's surgeon on a whaling vessel in the Arctic, and again in 1881 when he took a berth as medical officer on a cargo ship bound for Africa. During school vacations he worked as a medical assistant to augment the family's income. A passable student, he received his Bachelor of Medicine degree in 1881 and his doctorate in 1885. In 1882, he set up a small and only modestly successful practice in Southsea, England.

To fill the spare time between appointments, Conan Doyle appeased his literary penchant by writing stories. Throughout the course of his life, he would write many adventure and science fiction stories, historical romances, books on Spiritualism, and objective works, including, The War in South Africa: Its cause and Conduct (a widely circulated pamphlet denying British atrocities in the Boer War, for which he received his knighthood in 1902.

Thereafter, he penned down The Adventures of Sherlock Holmes, The Hound of the Baskervilles, which made him a much acclaimed author overnight. After such an illustrious career, he died in 1930.

Contents

Holmes

Dr. Watson

Dr. Mortimer

Sir Henry Baskerville

Dr. James Mortimer with Sherlock Holmes

One fine morning, Dr. Watson chanced to see a stick in the house of Sherlock Holmes. Just under the head was a broad silver band nearly an inch across. "To James Mortimer, M.R.C.S., from his friends of the C.C.H.," was engraved upon it, with the date "1884." It was just such a stick as the old-fashioned family practitioner used to carry -- dignified, solid and reassuring.

"Well, Watson, what do you make of it," asked Holmes.

"I think," said I, following as far as I could the methods of my companion, "that Dr. Mortimer is a successful, elderly medical man, well esteemed since those who know him give him this mark of their appreciation."

"Good!" said Holmes, "Excellent!"

"I think also that the probability is in favour of his being a country practitioner who does a great deal of his visiting on foot."

"Why so?"

"Because this stick, though originally a very handsome one has been so knocked about that I can hardly imagine a town practitioner carrying it. The thick-iron ferrule is worn down, so it is evident that he has done a great amount of walking with it."

"Perfectly sound!" said Holmes.

"And then again, there is the 'friends of the C.C.H. I

should guess that to be the Something Hunt, the local hunt to whose members he has possibly given some surgical assistance, and which has made him a small presentation in return."

"Interesting, though elementary," said he as he returned to his favourite corner of the settee, "There are certainly one or two indications upon the stick. It gives us the basis for several deductions."

"Has anything escaped me?" I asked with some self-importance, "I trust that there is nothing of consequence which I have overlooked."

"I am afraid, my dear Watson, that most of your conclusions were erroneous. When I said that you stimulated me I meant, to be frank, that in noting your fallacies I was occasionally guided towards the truth. Not that you are entirely wrong in this instance. The man is certainly a country practitioner. And he walks a good deal."

"Then I was right."

"To that extent."

"But that was all."

"No, no, my dear Watson, not all -- by no means all. I would suggest, for example, that a presentation to a doctor is more likely to come from a hospital than from a hunt, and that when the initials 'C.C.' are placed before that hospital the words 'Charing Cross' very naturally suggest themselves.'

"You may be right."

"The probability lies in that direction. And if we take this as a working hypothesis we have a fresh basis from which to start our construction of this unknown visitor."

"Well, then, supposing that 'C.C.H.' does stand for 'Charing Cross Hospital,' what further inferences may we draw?"

"Do none suggest themselves? You know my methods. Apply them!"

"I can only think of the obvious conclusion that the man has practised in town before going to the country."

I laughed incredulously as Sherlock Holmes leaned back in his settee and blew little wavering rings of smoke up to the ceiling.

"As to the latter part, I have no means of checking you," said I, "but at least it is not difficult to find out a few particulars about the man's age and professional career." From my small medical shelf I took down the Medical Directory and turned up the name. There were several Mortimers, but only one who could be our visitor. I read his record aloud.

"No mention of that local hunt, Watson," said Holmes with a mischievous smile, "but a country doctor, as you very astutely observed. I think that I am fairly justified in my inferences. As to the adjectives, I said, if I remember right, amiable, unambitious and absent-minded. It is my experience that it is only an amiable man in this world who receives testimonials, only an unambitious one who abandons a London career for the country, and only an absent-minded one who leaves his stick and not his visiting-card after waiting for an hour in your room."

"And the dog?"

"Has been in the habit of carrying this stick behind his master. Being a heavy stick the dog has held it tightly by the middle, and the marks of his teeth are very plainly visible. The dog's jaw, as shown in the space between these marks, is too broad in my opinion for a terrier and not broad enough for a mastiff. It may have been -- yes, by Jove, it is a curly-haired spaniel."

He had risen and paced the room as he spoke. Now

"No, this is my friend Dr Watson," said Sherlock.

he halted in the recess of the window. There was such a ring of conviction in his voice that I glanced up in surprise.

"My dear fellow, how can you possibly be so sure of that?"

"For the very simple reason that I see the dog himself on our very door-step, and there is the ring of its owner. Don't move, I beg you, Watson. He is a professional brother of yours, and your presence may be of assistance to me. Now is the dramatic moment of fate, Watson, when you hear a step upon the stair which is walking into your life, and you know not whether for good or ill. What does Dr. James Mortimer, the man of science, ask of Sherlock Holmes, the specialist in crime? Come in!"

The appearance of our visitor was a surprise to me, since I had expected a typical country practitioner. He was a very tall, thin man, with a long nose like a beak, which jutted out between two keen, grey eyes, set closely together and sparkling brightly from behind a pair of gold-rimmed glasses. He was clad in a professional but rather slovenly fashion, for his frock-coat was dingy and his trousers frayed. Though young, his long back was already bowed, and he walked with a forward thrust of his head and a general air of peering benevolence. As he entered, his eyes fell upon the stick in Holmes's hand, and he ran towards it with an exclamation of joy. "I am so very glad," said he, "I was not sure whether I had left it here or in the Shipping Office. I would not lose that stick for the world."

"A presentation, I see," said Holmes.

"Yes, sir."

"From Charing Cross Hospital?"

"From one or two friends there on the occasion of my marriage."

"Dear, dear, that's bad!" said Holmes, shaking his head.

Dr. Mortimer blinked through his glasses in mild astonishment.

"Why was it bad?"

"Only that you have disarranged our little deductions. Your marriage, you say?"

"Yes, sir. I married, and so left the hospital, and with it all hopes of a consulting practice. It was necessary to make a home of my own."

"Come, come, we are not so far wrong, after all," said Holmes, "And now, Dr. James Mortimer --"

"Mister, sir, Mister -- a humble M.R.C.S."

"And a man of precise mind, evidently."

"A dabbler in science, Mr. Holmes, a picker up of shells on the shores of the great unknown ocean. I presume that it is Mr. Sherlock Holmes whom I am addressing and not --"

"No, this is my friend Dr. Watson."

"Glad to meet you, sir. I have heard your name mentioned in connection with that of your friend. You interest me very much, Mr. Holmes. I had hardly expected so delicate a skull or such well-marked development on your skull. Would you have any objection to my running my finger across your skull? A cast of your skull, sir, until the original is available, would be an ornament to any anthropological museum. It is not my intention to be fulsome, but I confess that I covet your skull."

Sherlock Holmes waved our strange visitor into a chair. "You are an enthusiast in your line of thought, I perceive, sir, as I am in mine," said he, "I observe from your forefinger that you make your own cigarettes. Have no hesitation in lighting one."

The man drew out paper and tobacco and twirled the one up in the other with surprising dexterity. He had long, quivering fingers as agile and restless as the antennae of an insect.

Holmes was silent, but his little darting glances showed me the interest which he took in our curious companion.

"I presume, sir," said he at last, "that it was not merely for the purpose of examining my skull that you have done me the honour to call here last night and again to-day?"

"No, sir, no; though I am happy to have had the opportunity of doing that as well. I came to you, Mr. Holmes, because I recognized that I am myself an unpractical man and because I am suddenly confronted with a most serious and extraordinary problem. Recognizing, as I do, that you are the second highest expert in Europe."

"Indeed, sir! May I inquire who has the honour to be the first?" asked Holmes with some eagerness.

"To the man of precisely scientific mind the work of Monsieur Bertillon must always appeal strongly."

"Then had you not better consult him?"

"I said, sir, to the precisely scientific mind. But as a practical man of affairs, it is acknowledged that you stand alone. I trust, sir, that I have not inadvertently..."

"Just a little," said Holmes, "I think, Dr. Mortimer, you would do wisely if without more ado you would kindly tell me plainly what the exact nature of the problem is in which you demand my assistance."

Footprints of Hound

"I have in my pocket a manuscript," said Dr. James Mortimer.

"I observed it as you entered the room," said Holmes.

"It is an old manuscript."

"Early eighteenth century, unless it is a forgery."

"How can you say that, sir?"

"You have presented an inch or two of it to my examination all the time that you have been talking. It would be a poor expert who could not give the date of a document within a decade or so. You may possibly have read my little monograph upon the subject. I put that at 1730."

"The exact date is 1742." Dr. Mortimer drew it from his breast-pocket. "This family paper was committed to my care by Sir Charles Baskerville, whose sudden and tragic death some three months ago created so much excitement in Devonshire. I may say that I was his personal friend as well as his medical attendant. He was a strong-minded man, sir, shrewd, practical, and as unimaginative as I am myself. Yet he took this document very seriously, and his mind was prepared for just such an end as did eventually overtake him."

Holmes stretched out his hand for the manuscript and flattened it upon his knee.

"You will observe, Watson, the alternative use of the

long *s* and the short. It is one of several indications which enabled me to fix the date."

I looked over his shoulder at the yellow paper and the faded script. At the head was written: "Baskerville Hall," and below in large, scrawling figures: "1742."

"It appears to be a statement of some sort."

"Yes, it is a statement of a certain legend which runs in the Baskerville family."

"But I understand that it is something more modern and practical upon which you wish to consult me."

"Most modern. A most practical, pressing matter, which must be decided within twenty-four hours. But the manuscript is short and is intimately connected with the affair. With your permission I will read it to you."

Holmes leaned back in his chair, placed his finger-tips together, and closed his eyes, with an air of resignation. Dr. Mortimer turned the manuscript to the light and read in a high, cracking voice.

When Dr. Mortimer had finished reading this singular narrative he pushed his spectacles up on his forehead and stared across at Mr. Sherlock Holmes. The latter yawned and tossed the end of his cigarette into the fire.

"Well," said he.

"Do you not find it interesting?"

"To a collector of fairy tales."

Dr. Mortimer drew a folded newspaper out of his pocket.

"Now, Mr. Holmes, we will give you something a little more recent. This is the Devon County Chronicle of June 14th of this year. It is a short account of the facts elicited at the death of Sir Charles Baskerville which occurred a few days before that date."

My friend leaned a little forward and his expression became intent.

Dr. James Mortimer thus stated, "The facts of the case are simple. Sir Charles Baskerville was in the habit every night before going to bed of walking down the famous Yew Alley of Baskerville Hall. The evidence of the Barrymores shows that this had been his custom. On the fourth of June Sir Charles had declared his intention of starting next day for London, and had ordered Barrymore to prepare his luggage. That night, he went out as usual for his nocturnal walk, in the course of which he was in the habit of smoking a cigar. He never returned. At twelve o'clock Barrymore, finding the hall door still open, became alarmed, and, lighting a lantern, went in search of his master. The day had been wet, and Sir Charles's footmarks were easily traced down the alley. Halfway down this walk, there is a gate which leads out on to the moor. There were indications that Sir Charles had stood for some little time here. He then proceeded down the alley, and it was at the far end of it that his body was discovered. One fact which has not been explained is the statement of Barrymore that his master's footprints altered their character from the time he passed the moor-gate, and that he appeared from thence onward to have been walking upon his toes. One Murphy, a gipsy horse-dealer, was on the moor at no great distance at the time, but he appears by his own confession to have been the worse for drink. He declares that he heard cries but is unable to state from what direction they came. No signs of violence were to be discovered upon Sir Charles's person, and though the doctor's evidence pointed to an almost incredible facial distortion -- so great that Dr. Mortimer refused at first to believe that it was indeed his friend and patient who lay before him -- it was explained that that is a symptom which is not unusual in cases of dyspnoea and death from cardiac exhaustion. This explanation was borne out by the post-mortem examination, which showed long-standing organic disease, and the coroner's jury returned a verdict in accordance with the medical evidence. It is well that this is so, for it is obviously of the utmost importance that Sir Charles's heir should settle at the Hall and continue the good work which has been so sadly interrupted. Had the prosaic finding of the coroner not finally put an end to the romantic stories which have been whispered in connection with the affair, it might have been difficult to find a tenant for Baskerville Hall. It is understood that the next of kin is Mr. Henry Baskerville, if he be still alive, the son of Sir Charles Baskerville's younger brother. The young man when last heard of was in America, and inquiries are being instituted with a view to informing him of his good fortune."

Dr. Mortimer refolded his paper and replaced it in his pocket.

"Those are the public facts, Mr. Holmes, in connection with the death of Sir Charles Baskerville."

"I must thank you," said Sherlock Holmes, "for calling my attention to a case which certainly presents some features of interest. I had observed some newspaper comment at the time, but I was exceedingly preoccupied by that little affair of the Vatican cameos, and in my anxiety to oblige the Pope I lost touch with several interesting English cases. This article, you say, contains all the public facts."

"It does."

"Then let me have the private ones." He leaned back, put his finger-tips together, and assumed his most impassive and judicial expression.

Dr. Mortimer looked at his watch.

"On the night of Sir Charles's death Barrymore the butler who made the discovery, sent Perkins the groom on horseback to me, and as I was sitting up late I was able to reach Baskerville Hall within an hour of the event. I checked and corroborated all the facts which were mentioned at the inquest. I followed the footsteps down the Yew Alley. I saw the spot at the moor-gate where he seemed to have waited. I remarked the change in the shape of the prints after that point. I noted that there were no other footsteps save those of Barrymore on the soft gravel, and finally I carefully examined the body, which had not been touched until my arrival. Sir Charles lay on his face, his arms out, his fingers dug into the ground, and his features convulsed with some strong emotion to such an extent that I could hardly have sworn to his identity. There was certainly no physical injury of any kind. But one false statement was made by Barrymore at the inquest. He said that there were no traces upon the ground round the body. He did not observe any. But I did -- some little distance off, but fresh and clear."

"Footprints?"

"Footprints. "

"A man's or a woman's?"

Dr. Mortimer looked strangely at us for an instant, and his voice sank almost to a whisper as he answered:

"Mr. Holmes, they were the footprints of a gigantic hound!"

Sherlock Holmes struck his hand against his knee with an impatient gesture.

"If I had only been there!" he cried, "It is evidently a case of extraordinary interest, and one which presented immense opportunities to the scientific expert. That gravel page upon which I might have read so much has been long ere this smudged by the rain and defaced by the clogs of curious peasants. Oh, Dr. Mortimer, Dr. Mortimer, to think that you should not have called me in! You have indeed much to answer for."

"I could not call you in, Mr. Holmes, without disclosing these facts to the world, and I have already given my reasons for not wishing to do so. Besides, besides --"

"Why do you hesitate?"

"There is a realm in which the most acute and most experienced of detectives is helpless."

"You mean that the thing is supernatural."

"I did not positively say so."

"No, but you evidently think it."

"Since the tragedy, Mr. Holmes, there have come to my ears several incidents which are hard to reconcile with the settled order of Nature."

"For example?"

"I find that before the terrible event occurred several people had seen a creature upon the moor which corresponds with this Baskerville demon, and which could not possibly be any animal known to science. They all agreed that it was a huge creature, luminous, ghastly, and spectral. I have cross-examined these men, one of them a hard-headed countryman, one a farrier, and one a moorland farmer, who all tell the same story of this dreadful apparition, exactly corresponding to the hell-hound of the legend. I assure you that there is a reign of terror in the district, and that it is a hardy man who will cross the moor at night."

"And you, a trained man of science, believe it to be supernatural?"

"I do not know what to believe."

Holmes shrugged off his shoulders.

"I have hitherto confined my investigations to this world," said he, "In a modest way I have combated evil, but to take on the Father of Evil himself would, perhaps, be too ambitious a task. Yet, you must admit that the footmark is material."

"The original hound was material enough to tug a man's throat out, and yet he was diabolical as well."

"I see that you have quite gone over to the supernaturalists. But now, Dr. Mortimer, tell me this. If you hold these views, why have you come to consult me at all? You tell me in the same breath that it is useless to investigate Sir Charles's death, and that you desire me to do it."

"I did not say that I desired you to do it."

"Then, how can I assist you?"

"By advising me as to what I should do with Sir Henry Baskerville, who arrives at Waterloo Station" -- Dr. Mortimer looked at his watch -- "in exactly one hour and a quarter."

"He being the heir?"

"Yes. On the death of Sir Charles we inquired for this young gentleman and found that he had been farming in Canada. From the accounts which have reached us he is an excellent fellow in every way. I speak now not as a medical man but as a trustee and executor of Sir Charles's will."

"There is no other claimant, I presume?"

"None. The only other kinsman whom we have been able to trace was Rodger Baskerville, the youngest of three brothers of whom poor Sir Charles was the elder. The second brother, who died young, is the father of this lad Henry. The third, Rodger, was the black sheep of the family. He came of the old masterful Baskerville strain and was the very image, they tell me, of the family picture of old Hugo. He made England too hot to hold him, fled to Central America, and died there in 1876 of yellow fever. Henry is the last of the Baskervilles. In one hour and five minutes, I meet him at Waterloo Station. I have had a wire that he arrived at Southampton this morning. Now, Mr. Holmes, what would you advise me to do with him?"

"Why should he not go to the home of his fathers?"

"It seems natural, does it not? And yet, consider that every Baskerville who goes there meets with an evil fate. I feel sure that if Sir Charles could have spoken with me before his death he would have warned me against bringing this, the last of the old race, and the heir to great wealth, to that deadly place. And yet, it cannot be denied that the prosperity of the whole poor, bleak countryside depends upon his presence. All the good work which has been done by Sir Charles will crash to the ground if there is no tenant of the Hall. I fear lest I should be swayed too much by my own obvious interest in the matter, and that is why I bring the case before you and ask for your advice."

Holmes considered for a little time.

"Put into plain words, the matter is this," said he, "In your opinion, there is a diabolical agency which makes Dartmoor an unsafe abode for a Baskerville -- that is your opinion?"

"At least I might go the length of saying that there is some evidence that this may be so."

"Exactly. But surely, if your supernatural theory be correct, it could work the young man evil in London as easily as in Devonshire. A devil with merely local powers like a parish vestry would be too inconceivable a thing."

"You put the matter more flippantly, Mr. Holmes, than you would probably do if you were brought into personal contact with these things. Your advice, then, as I understand it, is that the young man will be as safe in Devonshire as in London. He comes in fifty minutes. What would you recommend?"

"I recommend, sir, that you take a cab, call off your spaniel who is scratching at my front door, and proceed to Waterloo to meet Sir Henry Baskerville."

"And then?"

"And then you will say nothing to him at all until I have made up my mind about the matter."

"How long will it take you to make up your mind?"

"Twenty-four hours. At ten o'clock to-morrow, Dr. Mortimer, I will be much obliged to you if you will call upon me here, and it will be of help to me in my plans for the future if you will bring Sir Henry Baskerville with you."

"I will do so, Mr. Holmes."

Holmes Interrogates Sir Henry Baskerville

Our breakfast table was cleared early, and Holmes waited in his dressing-gown for the promised interview. Our clients were punctual to their appointment, for the clock had just struck ten when Dr. Mortimer was shown up, followed by the young baronet. The latter was a small, alert, dark-eyed man about thirty years of age, very sturdily built, with thick black eyebrows and a strong, pugnacious face. He wore a ruddy-tinted tweed suit and had the weather-beaten appearance of one who has spent most of his time in the open air, and yet there was something in his steady eye and the quiet assurance of his bearing which indicated the gentleman.

"This is Sir Henry Baskerville," said Dr. Mortimer.

"Why, yes," said he, "and the strange thing is, Mr. Sherlock Holmes, that if my friend here had not proposed coming round to you this morning I should have come on my own account. I understand that you think out little puzzles, and I've had one this morning which wants more thinking out than I am able to give it."

"Please take a seat, Sir Henry. Do I understand you to say that you have yourself had some remarkable experience since you arrived in London?"

"Nothing of much importance, Mr. Holmes. Only a

joke, as like as not. It was this letter, if you can call it a letter, which reached me this morning."

He laid an envelope upon the table, and we all bent over it. It was of common quality, greyish in colour. The address, "Sir Henry Baskerville, Northumberland Hotel," was printed in rough characters; the post-mark "Charing Cross," and the date of posting the preceding evening.

"Who knew that you were going to the Northumberland Hotel?" asked Holmes, glancing keenly across at our visitor.

"No one could have known. We only decided after I had met Dr. Mortimer."

"But Dr. Mortimer was no doubt already stopping there?"

"No, I had been staying with a friend," said the doctor, "There was no possible indication that we intended to go to this hotel."

"Hum! Someone seems to be very deeply interested in your movements." Out of the envelope he took a half-sheet of foolscap paper folded into four. This he opened and spread flat upon the table. Across the middle of it, a single sentence had been formed by the expedient of pasting printed words upon it. It ran:

As you value your life or your reason, keep away from the moor. The word "moor" only was printed in ink.

"Now," said Sir Henry Baskerville, "perhaps you will tell me, Mr. Holmes, what in thunder is the meaning of that, and who it is that takes so much interest in my affairs?"

"What do you make of it, Dr. Mortimer? You must allow that there is nothing supernatural about this, at any rate."

"What business?" asked Sir Henry sharply.

"No, sir, but it might very well come from someone who was convinced that the business is supernatural."

"What business?" asked Sir Henry sharply, "It seems to me that all you gentlemen know a great deal more than I do about my own affairs."

"You shall share our knowledge before you leave this room, Sir Henry. I promise you that," said Sherlock Holmes, "We will confine ourselves for the present with your permission to this very interesting document, which must have been put together and posted yesterday evening. Have you yesterday's Times, Watson?"

"It is here in the corner."

"Might I trouble you for it -- the inside page, please, with the leading articles?" He glanced swiftly over it, running his eyes up and down the columns. "Capital article this on free trade. Permit me to give you an extract from it."

"You may be cajoled into imagining that your own special trade or your own industry will be encouraged by a protective tariff, but it stands to reason that such legislation must in the long run keep away wealth from the country, diminish the value of our imports, and lower the general conditions of life in this island."

"What do you think of that, Watson?" cried Holmes in high glee, rubbing his hands together with satisfaction, "Don't you think that is an admirable sentiment?"

Dr. Mortimer looked at Holmes with an air of professional interest, and Sir Henry Baskerville turned a pair of puzzled dark eyes upon me.

"I don't know much about the tariff and things of that kind," said he, "but it seems to me we've got a bit off the trail so far as that note is concerned."

"On the contrary, I think we are particularly hot upon the trail, Sir Henry. Watson here knows more about my methods than you do, but I fear that even he has not quite grasped the significance of this sentence."

"No, I confess that I see no connection."

"And yet, my dear Watson, there is so very close a connection that the one is extracted out of the other. 'You,' 'your,' 'life,' 'reason,' 'value,' 'keep away,' 'from the.' Don't you see now whence these words have been taken?"

"By thunder, you're right! Well, if that isn't smart!" cried Sir Henry.

"If any possible doubt remained, it is settled by the fact that 'keep away' and 'from the' are cut out in one piece."

"Well, now -- so it is!"

"Really, Mr. Holmes, this exceeds anything which I could have imagined," said Dr. Mortimer, gazing at my friend in amazement, "I could understand anyone saying that the words were from a newspaper; but that you should name which, and add that it came from the leading article, is really one of the most remarkable things which I have ever known. How did you do it?"

"I presume, Doctor, that you could tell the skull of a Negro from that of an Esquimaux?"

"Most certainly."

"But how?"

"Because that is my special hobby. The differences are obvious. The supra-orbital crest, the facial angle, the maxillary curve, the --"

"But this is my special hobby, and the differences are equally obvious. There is as much difference to my eyes between the leaded bourgeois type of a Times article and the slovenly print of an evening half-penny paper as there could be between your Negro and your Esquimaux. The detection of types is one of the most elementary branches of knowledge to the special expert in crime, though I confess that once when I was very young I confused the Leeds Mercury with the Western Morning News. But a Times leader is entirely distinctive, and these words could have been taken from nothing else. As it was done yesterday the strong probability was that we should find the words in yesterday's issue."

"So far as I can follow you, then, Mr. Holmes," said Sir Henry Baskerville, "someone cut out this message with a scissors."

"Nail-scissors," said Holmes, "You can see that it was a very short-bladed scissors, since the cutter had to take two snips over 'keep away.' "

"That is so. Someone, then, cut out the message with a pair of short-bladed scissors, pasted it with paste."

"Gum," said Holmes.

"With gum on to the paper. But I want to know why the word 'moor' should have been written."

"Because he could not find it in print. The other words were all simple and might be found in any issue, but 'moor' would be less common."

"Why, of course, that would explain it. Have you read anything else in this message, Mr. Holmes?"

"There are one or two indications, and yet the utmost pains have been taken to remove all clues. The address, you observe, is printed in rough characters. But the Times is a paper which is seldom found in any hands but those of the highly educated. We may take it, therefore,

"Have you read anything else
in this message, Mr. Holmes?"

that the letter was composed by an educated man who wished to pose as an uneducated one, and his effort to conceal his own writing suggests that that writing might be known, or come to be known, by you. Again, you will observe that the words are not gummed on in an accurate line, but that some are much higher than others. 'Life,' for example, is quite out of its proper place. That may point to carelessness or it may point to agitation and hurry upon the part of the cutter. On the whole, I incline to the latter view, since the matter was evidently important, and it is unlikely that the composer of such a letter would be careless. If he were in a hurry, it opens up the interesting question why he should be in a hurry, since any letter posted up to early morning would reach Sir Henry before he would leave his hotel. Did the composer fear an interruption...and from whom?"

"We are coming now rather into the region of guesswork," said Dr. Mortimer.

"Say, rather, into the region where we balance probabilities and choose the most likely. It is the scientific use of the imagination, but we have always some material basis on which to start our speculation. Now, you would call it a guess, no doubt, but I am almost certain that this address has been written in a hotel."

"How in the world can you say that?"

"If you examine it carefully, you will see that both the pen and the ink have given the writer trouble. The pen has spluttered twice in a single word and has run dry three times in a short address, showing that there was very little ink in the bottle. Now, a private pen or ink-bottle is seldom allowed to be in such a state, and the combination of the two must be quite rare. But you know the hotel ink and the hotel pen, where it is rare to get anything else. Yes, I have very little hesitation in saying that could we examine the waste-paper baskets of the hotels around Charing Cross until we found the remains of the mutilated Times leader we could lay our hands straight upon the person who sent this singular message. Halloa! Halloa! What's this?"

He was carefully examining the foolscap, upon which the words were pasted, holding it only an inch or two from his eyes.

"Well?"

"Nothing," said he, throwing it down, "It is a blank halfsheet of paper, without even a water-mark upon it. I think we have drawn as much as we can from this curious letter; and now, Sir Henry, has anything else of interest happened to you since you have been in London."

"Why, no, Mr. Holmes. I think not."

"You have not observed anyone follow or watch you?"

"I seem to have walked right into the thick of a dime novel," said our visitor, "Why in thunder should anyone follow or watch me?"

"We are coming to that. You have nothing else to report to us before we go into this matter?"

"Well, it depends upon what you think worth reporting."

"I think anything out of the ordinary routine of life well worth reporting."

Sir Henry smiled.

"I don't know much of British life yet, for I have spent nearly all my time in the States and in Canada. But I hope that to lose one of your boots is not part of the ordinary routine of life over here."

"You have lost one of your boots?"

"My dear sir," cried Dr. Mortimer, "it is only mislaid. You will find it when you return to the hotel. What is the use of troubling Mr. Holmes with the trifles of this kind?"

"Well, he asked me for anything outside the ordinary routine."

"Exactly," said Holmes, "however foolish the incident may seem. You have lost one of your boots, you say?"

"Well, mislaid it, anyhow. I put them both outside my door last night, and there was only one in the morning. I could get no sense out of the chap who cleans them. The worst of it is that I only bought the pair last night in the Strand, and I have never had them on."

"If you have never worn them, why did you put them out to be cleaned?"

"They were tan boots and had never been varnished. That was why I put them out."

"Then I understand that on your arrival in London yesterday, you went out at once and bought a pair of boots?"

"I did a good deal of shopping. Dr. Mortimer here went round with me. You see, if I am to be squire down there I must dress the part, and it may be that I have got a little careless in my ways out West. Among other things I bought these brown boots -- gave six dollars for them -- and had one stolen before ever I had them on my feet."

"It seems a singularly useless thing to steal," said Sherlock Holmes, "I confess that I share Dr. Mortimer's belief that it will not be long before the missing boot is found."

"And, now, gentlemen," said the baronet with decision,

"it seems to me that I have spoken quite enough about the little that I know. It is time that you kept your promise and gave me a full account of what we are all driving at."

"Your request is a very reasonable one," Holmes answered, "Dr. Mortimer, I think you could not do better than to tell your story as you told it to us."

Thus encouraged, our scientific friend drew his papers from his pocket and presented the whole case as he had done upon the morning before. Sir Henry Baskerville listened with the deepest attention and with an occasional exclamation of surprise.

Holmes Threads the Events

"On the whole," said Holmes, "I think that your decision is a wise one. I have ample evidence that you are being dogged in London, and amid the millions of this great city it is difficult to discover who these people are or what their object can be. If their intentions are evil, they might do you a mischief, and we should be powerless to prevent it. You did not know, Dr. Mortimer, that you were followed this morning from my house?"

Dr. Mortimer started violently.

"Followed! By whom?"

"That, unfortunately, is what I cannot tell you. Have you among your neighbours or acquaintances on Dartmoor any man with a black, full beard?"

"No -- or, let me see -- why, yes. Barrymore, Sir Charles's butler, is a man with a full, black beard."

"Ha! Where is Barrymore?"

"He is in charge of the Hall."

"We had best ascertain if he is really there, or if by any possibility he might be in London."

"How can you do that?"

"Give me a telegraph form. 'Is all ready for Sir Henry?' That will do. Address to Mr. Barrymore, Baskerville Hall. What is the nearest telegraph-office? Grimpen. Very good, we will send a second wire to the postmaster, Grimpen: 'Telegram to Mr. Barrymore to be delivered into his own hand. If absent, please return wire to Sir Henry Baskerville, Northumberland Hotel.' That should let us know before evening whether Barrymore is at his post in Devonshire or not."

"That's so," said Baskerville, "By the way, Dr. Mortimer, who is this Barrymore, anyhow?"

"He is the son of the old caretaker, who is dead. They have looked after the Hall for four generations now. So far as I know, he and his wife are as respectable a couple as any in the county."

"At the same time," said Baskerville, "it's clear enough that so long as there are none of the family at the Hall, these people have a mighty fine home and nothing to do."

"That is true."

"Did Barrymore profit at all by Sir Charles's will?" asked Holmes.

"He and his wife had five hundred pounds each."

"Ha! Did they know that they would receive this?"

"Yes; Sir Charles was very fond of talking about the provisions of his wlll."

"That is very interesting."

"I hope," said Dr. Mortimer, "that you do not look with suspicious eyes upon everyone who received a legacy from Sir Charles, for I also had a thousand pounds left to me."

"Indeed! And anyone else?"

"There were many insignificant sums to individuals, and a large number of public charities. The residue all went to Sir Henry."

"And how much was the residue?"

"Seven hundred and forty thousand pounds."

Holmes raised his eyebrows in surprise. "I had no idea that so gigantic a sum was involved," said he.

"Sir Charles had the reputation of being rich, but we did not know how very rich he was until we came to examine his securities. The total value of the estate was close on to a million."

"Dear me! It is a stake for which a man might well play a desperate game. And one more question, Dr. Mortimer. Supposing that anything happened to our young friend here -- you will forgive the unpleasant hypothesis -- who would inherit the estate?"

"Since Rodger Baskerville, Sir Charles's younger brother died unmarried, the estate would descend to the Desmonds, who are distant cousins. James Desmond is an elderly clergyman in Westmoreland."

"Thank you. These details are all of great interest. Have you met Mr. James Desmond?"

"Yes; he once came down to visit Sir Charles. He is a man of venerable appearance and of saintly life. I remember that he refused to accept any settlement from Sir Charles, though he pressed it upon him."

"And this man of simple tastes would be the heir to Sir Charles's thousands."

"He would be the heir to the estate because that is entailed. He would also be the heir to the money unless it were willed otherwise by the present owner, who can, of course, do what he likes with it."

"And have you made your will, Sir Henry?"

"No, Mr. Holmes, I have not. I've had no time, for it was only yesterday that I learnt how matters stood. But in any case, I feel that the money should go with the title and estate. That was my poor uncle's idea. How is the owner going to restore the glories of the Baskervilles if he has not money enough to keep up the property? House, land, and dollars must go together."

*"Barrymore, sir Charles's butler, is a
man with a full, black beard.*

"Quite so. Well, Sir Henry, I am of one mind with you as to the advisability of your going down to Devonshire without delay. There is only one provision which I must make. You certainly must not go alone."

"Dr. Mortimer returns with me."

"But Dr. Mortimer has his practice to attend to, and his house is miles away from yours. With all the goodwill in the world he may be unable to help you. No, Sir Henry, you must take with you someone, a trusty man, who will be always by your side."

"Is it possible that you could come yourself, Mr. Holmes?"

"If matters came to a crisis, I should endeavour to be present in person; but you can understand that, with my extensive consulting practice and with the constant appeals which reach me from many quarters, it is impossible for me to be absent from London for an indefinite time. At the present instant, one of the most revered names in England is being besmirched by a blackmailer, and only I can stop a disastrous scandal. You will see how impossible it is for me to go to Dartmoor."

"Whom would you recommend, then?"

Holmes laid his hand upon my arm.

"If my friend would undertake it, there is no man who is better worth having at your side when you are in a tight place. No one can say so more confidently than I."

The proposition took me completely by surprise, but before I had time to answer, Baskerville seized me by the hand and wrung it heartily.

"Well, now, that is real kind of you, Dr. Watson," said he, "You see how it is with me, and you know just as much about the matter as I do. If you will come down to Baskerville Hall and see me through, I'll never forget it."

The promise of adventure had always a fascination for me, and I was complimented by the words of Holmes and by the eagerness with which the baronet hailed me as a companion.

"I will come, with pleasure," said I, "I do not know how I could employ my time better."

"And you will report very carefully to me," said Holmes, "When a crisis comes, as it will do, I will direct how you shall act. I suppose that by Saturday all might be ready?"

"Would that suit Dr. Watson?"

"Perfectly."

"Then on Saturday, unless you hear to the contrary, we shall meet at the ten-thirty train from Paddington."

❏

Dr. Watson Visits Baskerville Hall

Sir Henry Baskerville and Dr. Mortimer were ready upon the appointed day, and we started as arranged for Devonshire. Mr. Sherlock Holmes drove with me to the station and gave me his last parting injunctions and advice.

"I will not bias your mind by suggesting theories or suspicions, Watson," said he, "I wish you simply to report facts in the fullest possible manner to me, and you can leave me to do the theorizing."

"What sort of facts?" I asked.

"Anything which may seem to have a bearing however indirect upon the case, and especially the relations between young Baskerville and his neighbours or any fresh particulars concerning the death of Sir Charles. I have made some inquiries myself in the last few days, but the results have, I fear, been negative. One thing only appears to be certain, and that is that Mr. James Desmond, who is the next heir, is an elderly gentleman of a very amiable disposition, so that this persecution does not arise from him. I really think that we may eliminate him entirely from our calculations. There remain the people who will actually surround Sir Henry Baskerville upon the moor."

"Would it not be well in the first place to get rid of this Barrymore couple?"

"Keep your revolver near you night and day."

"By no means. You could not make a greater mistake. If they are innocent, it would be a cruel injustice, and if they are guilty, we should be giving up all chance of bringing it home to them. No, no, we will preserve them upon our list of suspects. Then there is a groom at the Hall, if I remember right. There are two moorland farmers. There is our friend Dr. Mortimer, whom I believe to be entirely honest, and there is his wife, of whom we know nothing. There is this naturalist, Stapleton, and there is his sister, who is said to be a young lady of attractions. There is Mr. Frankland, of Lafter Hall, who is also an unknown factor. and there are one or two other neighbours. These are the folk who must be your very special study."

"I will do my best."

"You have arms, I suppose?"

"Yes, I thought it as well to take them."

"Most certainly. Keep your revolver near you night and day, and never relax your precautions."

Our friends had already secured a first-class carriage and were waiting for us upon the platform.

"No, we have no news of any kind," said Dr. Mortimer in answer to my friend's questions, "I can swear to one thing, and that is that we have not been shadowed during the last two days. We have never gone out without keeping a sharp watch, and no one could have escaped our notice."

"You have always kept together, I presume?"

"Except yesterday afternoon. I usually give up one day to pure amusement when I come to town, so I spent it at the Museum of the College of Surgeons."

"And I went to look at the folk in the park," said Baskerville, "But we had no trouble of any kind."

"It was imprudent, all the same," said Holmes, shaking his head and looking very grave, "I beg, Sir Henry, that you will not go about alone. Some great misfortune will befall you if you do. Did you get your other boot?"

"No, sir, it is gone for ever."

"Indeed. That is very interesting. Well, goodbye," he added as the train began to glide down the platform, "Bear in mind, Sir Henry, one of the phrases in that queer old legend which Dr. Mortimer has read to us and avoid the moor in those hours of darkness when the powers of evil are exalted."

I looked back at the plafform when we had left it far behind and saw the tall, austere figure of Holmes standing motionless and gazing after us.

The journey was a swift and pleasant one, and I spent it in making the more intimate acquaintance of my two companions and in playing with Dr. Mortimer's spaniel. In a very few hours, the brown earth had become ruddy, the brick had changed to granite, and red cows grazed in well-hedged fields where the lush grasses and more luxuriant vegetation spoke of a richer, if a damper, climate. Young Baskerville stared eagerly out of the window and cried aloud with delight as he recognized the familiar features of the Devon scenery.

"I've been over a good part of the world since I left it, Dr. Watson," said he, "but I have never seen a place to compare with it."

"l never saw a Devonshire man who did not swear by his county," I remarked.

"It depends upon the breed of men quite as much as on the county," said Dr. Mortimer, "A glance at our friend here reveals the rounded head of the Celt, which carries inside it the Celtic enthusiasm and power of attachment. Poor Sir Charles's head was of a very rare type, half Gaelic, half Ivernian in its characteristics. But you were very young when you last saw Baskerville Hall, were you not?"

"I was a boy in my teens at the time of my father's death and had never seen the Hall, for he lived in a little cottage on the South Coast. Thence I went straight to a friend in America. I tell you it is all as new to me as it is to Dr. Watson, and I'm as keen as possible to see the moor."

"Are you? Then your wish is easily granted, for there is your first sight of the moor," said Dr. Mortimer, pointing out of the carriage window.

Over the green squares of the fields and the low curve of a wood there rose in the distance a grey, melancholy hill, with a strange jagged summit, dim and vague in the distance, like some fantastic landscape in a dream. Baskerville sat for a long time his eyes fixed upon it, and I read upon his eager face how much it meant to him, this first sight of that strange spot where the men of his blood had held sway so long and left their mark so deep. There he sat, with his tweed suit and his American accent, in the corner of a prosaic railway-carriage, and yet as I looked at his dark and expressive face I felt more than ever how true a descendant he was of that long line of high-blooded, fiery and masterful men. There were pride, valour and strength in his thick brows, his sensitive nostrils, and his large hazel eyes. If on that forbidding moor a difficult and dangerous quest should lie before us, this was at least a comrade for whom one might venture to take a risk with the certainty that he would bravely share it.

The train pulled up at a small wayside station and we

The train pulled up at a small station and we all descended.

all descended. Outside, beyond the low, white fence, a wagonette with a pair of cobs was waiting. Our coming was evidently a great event, for station-master and porters clustered round us to carry out our luggage. It was a sweet, simple country spot, but I was surprised to observe that by the gate there stood two soldierly men in dark uniforms who leaned upon their short rifles and glanced keenly at us as we passed. The coachman, a hardfaced, gnarled little fellow, saluted Sir Henry Baskerville, and in a few minutes we were flying swiftly down the broad, white road. Rolling pasture lands curved upward on either side of us, and old gabled houses peeped out from amid the thick green foliage, but behind the peaceful and sunlit countryside there rose ever, dark against the evening sky, the long, gloomy curve of the moor, broken by the jagged and sinister hills.

The wagonette swung round into a side road, and we curved upward through deep lanes worn by centuries of wheels, high banks on either side, heavy with dripping moss and fleshy hart's-tongue ferns. Bronzing bracken and mottled bramble gleamed in the light of the sinking sun. Still steadily rising, we passed over a narrow granite bridge and skirted a noisy stream which gushed swiftly down, foaming and roaring amid the grey boulders. Both road and stream wound up through a valley dense with scrub oak and fir. At every turn Baskerville gave an exclamation of delight, looking eagerly about him and asking countless questions. To his eyes all seemed beautiful, but to me a tinge of melancholy lay upon the countryside, which bore so clearly the mark of the waning year. Yellow leaves carpeted the lanes and fluttered down upon us as we passed. The rattle of our wheels died away as we drove through the drifts of rotting vegetation -- sad gifts, as it seemed to me, for Nature to throw before the carriage of the returning heir of the Baskervilles.

"Halloa!" cried Dr. Mortimer, "what is this?"

A steep curve of heath-clad land, an outlying spur of the moor, lay in front of us. On the summit, hard and clear like an equestrian statue upon its pedestal, was a mounted soldier, dark and stern, his rifle poised ready over his forearm. He was watching the road along which we travelled.

"What is this, Perkins?" asked Dr. Mortimer.

Our driver half turned in his seat.

"There's a convict escaped from Princetown, sir. He's been out three days now, and the warders watch every road and every station, but they've had no sight of him yet. The farmers about here don't like it, sir, and that's a fact."

"Well, I understand that they get five pounds if they can give information."

"Yes, sir, but the chance of five pounds is but a poor thing compared to the chance of having your throat cut. You see, it isn't like any ordinary convict. This is a man that would stick at nothing."

"Who is he, then?"

"It is Selden, the Notting Hill murderer."

I remembered the case well, for it was one in which Holmes had taken an interest on account of the peculiar ferocity of the crime and the wanton brutality which had marked all the actions of the assassin. The commutation of his death sentence had been due to some doubts as to his complete sanity, so atrocious was his conduct. Our wagonette had topped a rise and in front of us rose the huge expanse of the moor, mottled with gnarled and craggy caims and tors. A cold wind swept down from it and set us shivering. Somewhere there, on that desolate plain, was lurking this fiendish man, hiding in a burrow like a wild beast, his heart full of malignancy against the whole race which had cast him out. It needed but this to complete the grim suggestiveness of the barren waste, the chilling wind, and the darkling sky. Even Baskerville fell silent and pulled his overcoat more closely around him.

We had left the fertile country behind and beneath us. We looked back on it now, the slanting rays of a low sun turning the streams to threads of gold and glowing on the red earth new turned by the plough and the broad tangle of the woodlands. The road in front of us grew bleaker and wilder over huge russet and olive slopes, sprinkled with giant boulders. Now and then we passed a moorland cottage, walled and roofed with stone, with no creeper to break its harsh outline. Suddenly we looked down into a cuplike depression, patched with stunted oaks and fus which had been twisted and bent by the fury of years of storm. Two high, narrow towers rose over the trees. The driver pointed with his whip.

"Baskerville Hall," said he.

Its master had risen and was staring with flushed cheeks and shining eyes. A few minutes later, we had reached the lodgegates, a maze of fantastic tracery in wrought iron, with weather-bitten pillars on either side, blotched with lichens, and summounted by the boars' heads of the Baskervilles. The lodge was a ruin of black granite and bared ribs of rafters, but facing it was a new building, half constructed, the first fruit of Sir Charles's South African gold.

Reports of Dr. Watson

Baskerville Hall, October 13th

My dear Holmes:

My previous letters and telegrams have kept you pretty well up to date as to all that has occurred in this most God-forsaken corner of the world. The longer one stays here, the more does the spirit of the moor sink into one's soul, its vastness, and also its grim charm. When you are once out upon its bosom, you have left all traces of modern England behind you, but, on the other hand, you are conscious everywhere of the homes and the work of the prehistoric people. On all sides of you as you walk are the houses of these forgotten folk, with their graves and the huge monoliths which are supposed to have marked their temples. As you look at their grey stone huts against the scarred hillsides you leave your own age behind you, and if you were to see a skin-clad, hairy man crawl out from the low door fitting a flint-tipped arrow on to the string of his bow, you would feel that his presence there was more natural than your own. The strange thing is that they should have lived so thickly on what must always have been most unfruitful soil. I am no antiquarian, but I could imagine that they were some unwarlike and harried race who were forced to accept that which none other would occupy.

All this, however, is foreign to the mission on which

you sent me and will probably be very uninteresting to your severely practical mind. I can still remember your complete indifference as to whether the sun moved round the earth or the earth round the sun. Let me, therefore, return to the facts concerning Sir Henry Baskerville.

If you have not had any report within the last few days it is because up to to-day there was nothing of importance to relate. Then a very surprising circumstance occurred, which I shall tell you in due course. But, first of all, I must keep you in touch with some of the other factors in the situation.

One of these, concerning which I have said little, is the escaped convict upon the moor. There is a strong reason now to believe that he has got right away, which is a considerable relief to the lonely householders of this district. A fortnight has passed since his flight, during which he has not been seen and nothing has been heard of him. It is surely inconceivable that he could have held out upon the moor during all that time. Of course, so far as his concealment goes there is no difficulty at all. Any one of these stone huts would give him a hiding-place. But there is nothing to eat unless he is to catch and slaughter one of the moor sheep. We think, therefore, that he has gone, and the outlying farmers sleep the better in consequence.

We are four able-bodied men in this household, so that we might take good care of ourselves, but I confess that I have had uneasy moments when I have thought of the Stapletons. They live miles from any help. There are one maid, an old manservant, the sister, and the brother, the latter not a very strong man. They would be helpless in the hands of a desperate fellow like this Notting Hill criminal if he could once effect an entrance. Both Sir

"We are four able-bodied men in this household."

Henry and I were concerned at their situation, and it was suggested that Perkins the groom should go over to sleep there, but Stapleton would not hear of it.

The fact is that our friend, the baronet, begins to display a considerable interest in our fair neighbour. It is not to be wondered at, for time hangs heavily in this lonely spot to an active man like him, and she is a very fascinating and beautiful woman. There is something tropical and exotic about her which forms a singular contrast to her cool and unemotional brother. Yet, he also gives the idea of hidden fires. He has certainly a very marked influence over her, for I have seen her continually glance at him as she talked as if seeking approbation for what she said. I trust that he is kind to her. There is a dry glitter in his eyes and a firm set of his thin lips, which goes with a positive and possibly a harsh nature. You would find him an interesting study.

He came over to call upon Baskerville on that first day, and the very next morning he took us both to show us the spot where the legend of the wicked Hugo is supposed to have had its origin. It was an excursion of some miles across the moor to a place which is so dismal that it might have suggested the story. We found a short valley between rugged tors which led to an open, grassy space flecked over with the white cotton grass. In the middle of it rose two great stones, worn and sharpened at the upper end until they looked like the huge corroding fangs of some monstrous beast. In every way it corresponded with the scene of the old tragedy. Sir Henry was much interested and asked Stapleton more than once whether he did really believe in the possibility of the interference of the supernatural in the affairs of men. He spoke lightly, but it was evident that he was very much in earnest. Stapleton was guarded in his replies, but it was easy to see that he said less than he might, and that he would not express his whole opinion out of consideration for the feelings of the baronet. He told us of similar cases, where families had suffered from some evil influence, and he left us with the impression that he shared the popular view upon the matter.

On our way back, we stayed for lunch at Merripit House, and it was there that Sir Henry made the acquaintance of Miss Stapleton. From the first moment that he saw her, he appeared to be strongly attracted by her, and I am much mistaken if the feeling was not mutual. He referred to her again and again on our walk home, and since then hardly a day has passed that we have not seen something of the brother and sister. They dine here to-night, and there is some talk of our going to them next week. One would imagine that such a match would be very welcome to Stapleton, and yet I have more than once caught a look of the strongest disapprobation in his face when Sir Henry has been paying some attention to his sister. He is much attached to her, no doubt, and would lead a lonely life without her, but it would seem the height of selfishness if he were to stand in the way of her making so brilliant a marriage. Yet, I am certain that he does not wish their intimacy to ripen into love, and I have several times observed that he has taken pains to prevent them from being tete-a-tete. By the way, your instructions to me never to allow Sir Henry to go out alone will become very much more onerous if a love-affair were to be added to our other difficulties. My popularity would soon suffer if I were to carry out your orders to the letter.

The other day -- Thursday, to be more exact -- Dr. Mortimer lunched with us. He has been excavating a barrow at Long Down and has got a prehistoric skull which fills him with great joy. Never was there such a single-minded enthusiast as he! The Stapletons came in afterwards, and the good doctor took us all to the Yew Alley at Sir Henry's request to show us exactly how everything occurred upon that fatal night. It is a long, dismal walk, the Yew Alley, between two high walls of clipped hedge, with a narrow band of grass upon either side. At the far end is an old tumble-down summer-house. Halfway down is the moorgate, where the old gentleman left his cigar-ash. It is a white wooden gate with a latch. Beyond it lies the wide moor. I remembered your theory of the affair and tried to picture all that had occurred. As the old man stood there, he saw something coming across the moor, something which terrified him so that he might lose his wits and ran and ran until he died of sheer horror and exhaustion. There was the long, gloomy tunnel down which he fled. And from what? A sheep-dog of the moor? Or a spectral hound, black, silent, and monstrous? Was there a human agency in the matter? Did the pale, watchful Barrymore know more than he cared to say? It was all dim and vague, but always there is the dark shadow of crime behind it.

From time to time Dr. Watson kept on writing to Sherlock Holmes about the events which took place in Baskerville Hall. In his second report, he wrote to Sherlock Holmes in the following manner as given on the next page.

Baskerville Hall, Oct. 15th

My dear Holmes,

If I was compelled to leave you without much news during the early days of my mission you must acknowledge that I am making up for lost time, and that events are now crowding thick and fast upon us. In my last report, I ended upon my top note with Barrymore at the window, and now I have quite a budget already which will, unless I am much mistaken, considerably surprise you. Things have taken a turn which I could not have anticipated. In some ways they have within the last forty-eight hours become much clearer and in some ways they have become more complicated. But I will tell you all and you shall judge for yourself.

Before breakfast on the morning following my adventure, I went down the corridor and examined the room in which Barrymore had been on the-night before. The western window through which he had stared so intently has, I noticed, one peculiarity above all other windows in the house -- it commands the nearest outlook on to the moor. There is an opening between two trees which enables one from this point of view to look right down upon it, while from all the other windows it is only a distant glimpse which can be obtained. It follows, therefore, that Barrymore, since only this window would serve the purpose, must have been looking out for something or somebody upon the moor. The night was very dark, so that I can hardly imagine how he could have hoped to see anyone. It had struck me that it was possible that some love intrigue was on foot. That would have accounted for his stealthy movements and also for the uneasiness of his wife. The man is a striking-looking fellow, very well equipped to steal the heart of a country girl, so that this theory might seem to have something to support it. That opening of the door which I had heard after I had returned to my room might mean that he had gone out to keep some clandestine appointment. So I reasoned with myself in the morning, and I tell you the direction of my suspicions, however much the result may have shown that they were unfounded.

But whatever the true explanation of Barrymore's movements might be, I felt that the responsibility of keeping them to myself until I could explain them was more than I could bear. I had an interview with the baronet in his study after breakfast, and I told him all that I had seen. He was less surprised than I had expected.

"I knew that Barrymore walked about nights, and I had a mind to speak to him about it," said he, "Two or three times I have heard hls steps in the passage, coming and going, just about the hour you name."

"Perhaps then he pays a visit every night to that particular window," I suggested.

"Perhaps he does. If so, we should be able to shadow him and see what it is that he is after. I wonder what your friend Holmes would do if he were here."

"I believe that he would do exactly what you now suggest," said I, "He would follow Barrymore and see what he did."

"Then we shall do it together."

"But surely he would hear us."

"The man is rather deaf, and in any case we must take our chance of that. We'll sit up in my room to-night and wait until he passes." Sir Henry rubbed his hands with pleasure, and it was evident that he hailed the adventure as a relief to his somewhat quiet life upon the moor.

*"I had an interview with the baronet
in his study after breakfast."*

The baronet has been in communication with the architect who prepared the plans for Sir Charles, and with a contractor from London, so that we may expect great changes to begin here soon. There have been decorators and furnishers up from Plymouth, and it is evident that our friend has large ideas and means to spare no pains or expense to restore the grandeur of his family. When the house is renovated and refurnished, all that he will need will be a wife to make it complete. Between ourselves there are pretty clear signs that this will not be wanting if the lady is willing, for I have seldom seen a man more infatuated with a woman than he is with our beautiful neighbour, Miss Stapleton. And yet the course of true love does not run quite as smoothly as one would under the circumstances expect. To-day, for example, its surface was broken by a very unexpected ripple, which has caused our friend considerable perplexity and annoyance.

After the conversation which I have quoted about Barrymore, Sir Henry put on his hat and prepared to go out. As a matter of course, I did the same.

"What, are you coming, Watson?" he asked, looking at me in a curious way.

"That depends on whether you are going on the moor," said I.

"Yes, I am."

"Well, you know what my instructions are. I am sorry to intrude, but you heard how earnestly Holmes insisted that I should not leave you, and especially that you should not go alone upon the moor."

Sir Henry put his hand upon my shoulder with a pleasant smile.

"My dear fellow," said he, "Holmes, with all his wisdom, did not foresee some things which have happened

since I have been on the moor. Do you understand me? I am sure that you are the last man in the world who would wish to be a spoil-sport. I must go out alone."

It put me in a most awkward position. I was at a loss what to say or what to do, and before I had made up my mind he picked up his cane and was gone.

But when I came to think the matter over, my conscience reproached me bitterly for having on any pretext allowed him to go out of my sight. I imagined what my feelings would be if I had to return to you and to confess that some misfortune had occurred through my disregard for your instructions. I assure you my cheeks flushed at the very thought. It might not even now be too late to overtake him, so I set off at once in the direction of Merripit House.

'Such are the adventures of last night, and you must acknowledge, my dear Holmes, that I have done you very well in the matter of a report. Much of what I tell you is no doubt quite irrelevant, but still I feel that it is best that I should let you have all the facts and leave you to select for yourself those which will be of most service to you in helping you to your conclusions. We are certainly making some progress. So far as the Barrymores go we have found the motive of their actions, and that has cleared up the situation very much. But the moor with its mysteries and its strange inhabitants remains as inscrutable as ever. Perhaps in my next I may be able to throw some light upon this as well. Best of all would it be if you could come down to us.

Watson Establishes
Two Important Facts

I was determined to reach the heart of the mystery. I had established two facts of great importance, the one that Mrs. Laura Lyons of Coombe Tracey had written to Sir Charles Baskerville and made an appointment with him at the very place and hour that he met his death, the other that the lurking man upon the moor was to be found among the stone huts upon the hillside. With these two facts in my possession I felt that either my intelligence or my courage must be deficient if I could not throw some further light upon these dark places.

I had no opportunity to tell the baronet what I had learnt about Mrs. Lyons upon the evening before, for Dr. Mortimer remained with him at cards until it was very late. At breakfast, however, I informed him about my discovery and asked him whether he would care to accompany me to Coombe Tracey. At first, he was very eager to come, but on second thoughts it seemed to both of us that if I went alone the results might be better. The more formal we made the visit the less information we might obtain. I left Sir Henry behind, therefore, not without some prickings of conscience, and drove off upon my new quest.

When I reached Coombe Tracey, I told Perkins to put up the horses, and I made inquiries for the lady whom

"One was Mr. Stapleton, a neighbour
and intimate friend of Sir Charles."

I had come to interrogate. I had no difficulty in finding her rooms, which were central and well appointed. A maid showed me in without ceremony, and as I entered the sitting-room a lady, who was sitting before a Remington typewriter, sprang up with a pleasant smile of welcome. Her face fell, however, when she saw that I was a stranger, and she sat down again and asked me the object of my visit.

The first impression left by Mrs. Lyons was one of extreme beauty. Her eyes and hair were of the same rich hazel colour, and her cheeks, though considerably freckled, were flushed with the exquisite bloom of the brunette, the dainty pink which lurks at the heart of the sulphur rose. Admiration was, I repeat, the first impression. But the second was criticism. There was something subtly wrong with the face, some coarseness of expression, some hardness, perhaps, of eye, some looseness of lip which marred its perfect beauty. But these, of course, are after-thoughts. At the moment, I was simply conscious that I was in the presence of a very handsome woman, and that she was asking me the reasons for my visit. I had not quite understood until that instant how delicate my mission was.

"I have the pleasure," said I, "of knowing your father." It was a clumsy introduction, and the lady made me feel it.

"There is nothing in common between my father and me," she said, "I owe him nothing, and his friends are not mine. If it were not for the late Sir Charles Baskerville and some other kind hearts I might have starved for all that my father cared."

"It was about the late Sir Charles Baskerville that I have come here to see you."

The freckles started out on the lady's face.

"What can I tell you about him?" she asked, and her fingers played nervously over the stops of her typewriter.

"You knew him, did you not?"

"I have already said that I owe a great deal to his kindness. If I am able to support myself it is largely due to the interest which he took in my unhappy situation."

"Did you correspond with him?"

The lady looked quickly up with an angry gleam in her hazel eyes.

"What is the object of these questions?" she asked sharply.

"The object is to avoid a public scandal. It is better that I should ask them here than that the matter should pass outside our control."

She was silent and her face was still very pale. At last she looked up with something reckless and defiant in her manner.

"Well, I'll answer," she said, "What are your questions?"

"Did you correspond with Sir Charles?"

"I certainly wrote to him once or twice to acknowledge his delicacy and his generosity."

"Have you the dates of those letters?"

"No."

"Have you ever met him?"

"Yes, once or twice, when he came into Coombe Tracey. He was a very retiring man, and he preferred to do good by stealth."

"But if you saw him so seldom and wrote so seldom, how did he know enough about your affairs to be able to help you, as you say that he has done?"

She met my difficulty with the utmost readiness.

"There were several gentlemen who knew my sad

The Hound of The Baskervilles—4

history and united to help me. One was Mr. Stapleton, a neighbour and intimate friend of Sir Charles's. He was exceedingly kind, and it was through him that Sir Charles learnt about my affairs."

I knew already that Sir Charles Baskerville had made Stapleton his almoner upon several occasions, so the lady's statement bore the impress of truth upon it.

"Did you ever write to Sir Charles asking him to meet you?" I continued.

Mrs. Lyons flushed with anger again.

"Really, sir, this is a very extraordinary question."

"I am sorry, madam, but I must repeat it."

"Then I answer, certainly not."

"Not on the very day of Sir Charles's death?"

The flush had faded in an instant, and a deathly face was before me. Her dry lips could not speak the "No" which I saw rather than heard.

"Surely your memory deceives you," said I, "I could even quote a passage of your letter. It ran 'Please, please, as you are a gentleman, burn this letter, and be at the gate by ten o'clock.'

I thought that she had fainted, but she recovered herself by a supreme effort.

"Is there no such thing as a gentleman?" she gasped.

"You do Sir Charles an injustice. He did burn the letter. But sometimes a letter may be legible even when burned. You acknowledge now that you wrote it?"

"Yes, I did write it," she cried, pouring out her soul in a torrent of words, "I did write it. Why should I deny it? I have no reason to be ashamed of it. I wished him to help me. I believed that if I had an interview I could gain his help, so I asked him to meet me."

"But why at such an hour?"

"I quoted the postscript. The latter had burned."

"Because I had only just learned that he was going to London next day and might be away for months. There were reasons why I could not get there earlier."

"But why a rendezvous in the garden instead of a visit to the house?"

"Do you think a woman could go alone at that hour to a bachelor's house?"

"Well, what happened when you did get there?"

"I never went."

"Mrs. Lyons!"

"No, I swear it to you on all I hold sacred. I never went. Something intervened to prevent my going."

"What was that?"

"That is a private matter. I cannot tell it."

"You acknowledge then that you made an appointment with Sir Charles at the very hour and place at which he met his death, but you deny that you kept the appointment."

"That is the truth."

Again and again, I cross-questioned her, but I could never get past that point.

"Mrs. Lyons," said I as I rose from this long and inconclusive interview, "you are taking a very great responsibility and putting yourself in a very false position by not making an absolutely clean breast of all that you know. If I have to call in the aid of the police you will find how seriously you are compromised. If your position is innocent, why did you in the first instance deny having written to Sir Charles upon that date?"

"Because I feared that some false conclusion might be drawn from it and that I might find myself involved in a scandal."

"And why were you so pressing that Sir Charles should destroy your letter?"

"If you have read the letter you will know."

"I did not say that I had read all the letter."

"You quoted some of it."

"I quoted the postscript. The letter had, as I said, been burned and it was not all legible. I ask you once again why it was that you were so pressing that Sir Charles should destroy this letter which he received on the day of his death."

"The matter is a very private one."

"The more reason why you should avoid a public investigation."

"I will tell you, then. If you have heard anything of my unhappy history you will know that I made a rash marriage and had reason to regret it."

"I have heard so much."

"My life has been one incessant persecution from a husband whom I abhor. The law is upon his side, and every day I am faced by the possibility that he may force me to live with him. At the time that I wrote this letter to Sir Charles I had learned that there was a prospect of my regaining my freedom if certain expenses could be met. It meant everything to me -- peace of mind, happiness, self-respect -- everything. I knew Sir Charles's generosity, and I thought that if he heard the story from my own lips he would help me."

"Then how is it that you did not go?"

"Because I received help in the interval from another source."

"Why then, did you not write to Sir Charles and explain this?"

"So I should have done had I not seen his death in the paper next morning."

The woman's story hung coherently together, and all

my questions were unable to shake it. I could only check it by finding if she had, indeed, instituted divorce proceedings against her husband at or about the time of the tragedy.

It was unlikely that she would dare to say that she had not been to Baskerville Hall if she really had been, for a trap would be necessary to take her there, and could not have returned to Coombe Tracey until the early hours of the morning. Such an excursion could not be kept secret. The probability was, therefore, that she was telling the truth, or, at least, a part of the truth. I came away baffled and disheartened. Once again, I had reached that dead wall which seemed to be built across every path by which I tried to get at the object of my mission. And yet the more I thought of the lady's face and of her manner the more I felt that something was being held back from me. Why should she turn so pale? Why should she fight against every admission until it was forced from her? Why should she have been so reticent at the time of the tragedy? Surely the explanation of all this could not be as innocent as she would have me believe. For the moment I could proceed no farther in that direction, but must turn back to that other clue which was to be sought for among the stone huts upon the moor.

Chapter 8

Holmes Joins Watson

One fine morning, I heard a well-known voice. For a moment or two I sat breathless, hardly able to believe my ears. Then my senses and my voice came back to me, while a crushing weight of responsibility seemed in an instant to be lifted from my soul. That cold, incisive, ironical voice could belong to but one man in all the world.

"Holmes!" I cried -- "Holmes!"

"Come out," said he, "and please be careful with the revolver."

I stooped under the rude lintel, and there he sat upon a stone outside, his gray eyes dancing with amusement as they fell upon my astonished features. He was thin and worn, but clear and alert, his keen face bronzed by the sun and roughened by the wind. In his tweed suit and cloth cap he looked like any other tourist upon the moor, and he had contrived, with that catlike love of personal cleanliness which was one of his characteristics, that his chin should be as smooth and his linen as perfect as if he were in Baker Street.

"I never was more glad to see anyone in my life," said I as I wrung him by the hand.

"Or more astonished, eh?"

"Well, I must confess to it."

"The surprise was not all on one side, I assure you.

I had no idea that you had found my occasional retreat, still less that you were inside it, until I was within twenty paces of the door."

"My footprint, I presume?"

"No, Watson, I fear that I could not undertake to recognize your footprint amid all the footprints of the world. If you seriously desire to deceive me you must change your tobacconist; for when I see the stub of a cigarette marked Bradley, Oxford Street, I know that my friend Watson is in the neighbourhood. You will see it there beside the path. You threw it down, no doubt, at that supreme moment when you charged into the empty hut."

"Exactly."

"I thought as much -- and knowing your admirable tenacity I was convinced that you were sitting in ambush, a weapon within reach, waiting for the tenant to return. So you actually thought that I was the criminal?"

"I did not know who you were, but I was determined to find out."

"Excellent, Watson! And how did you localize me? You saw me, perhaps, on the night of the convict hunt, when I was so imprudent as to allow the moon to rise behind me?"

"Yes, I saw you then."

"And have no doubt searched all the huts until you came to this one?"

"No, your boy had been observed, and that gave me a guide where to look."

"The old gentleman with the telescope, no doubt. I could not make it out when first I saw the light flashing upon the lens." He rose and peeped into the hut. "Ha, I see that Cartwright has brought up some supplies.

"No, your boy had been observed, and that gave me a guide where to look."

What's this paper? So you have been to Coombe Tracey, have you?"

"Yes."

"To see Mrs. Laura Lyons?"

"Exactly."

"Well done! Our researches have evidently been running on parallel lines, and when we unite our results I expect we shall have a fairly full knowledge of the case."

"Well, I am glad from my heart that you are here, for indeed the responsibility and the mystery were both becoming too much for my nerves. But how in the name of wonder did you come here, and what have you been doing? I thought that you were in Baker Street working out that case of blackmailing."

"That was what I wished you to think."

"Then you use me, and yet do not trust me!" I cried with some bitterness. "I think that I have deserved better at your hands, Holmes."

"My dear fellow, you have been invaluable to me in this as in many other cases, and I beg that you will forgive me if I have seemed to play a trick upon you. In truth, it was partly for your own sake that I did it, and it was my appreciation of the danger which you ran which led me to come down and examine the matter for myself. Had I been with Sir Henry and you it is confident that my point of view would have been the same as yours, and my presence would have warned our very formidable opponents to be on their guard. As it is, I have been able to get about as I could not possibly have done had I been living in the Hall, and I remain an unknown factor in the business, ready to throw in all my weight at a critical moment."

"But why did you keep me in the dark?"

"For you to know could not have helped us and might possibly have led to my discovery. You would have wished to tell me something, or in your kindness you would have brought me out some comfort or other, and so an unnecessary risk would be run. I brought Cartwright down with me -- you remember the little chap at the Express Office -- and he has seen after my simple wants: a loaf of bread and a clean collar. What does man want more? He has given me an extra pair of eyes upon a very active pair of feet, and both have been invaluable."

"Then my reports have all been wasted!" -- My voice trembled as I recalled the pains and the pride with which I had composed them.

Holmes took a bundle of papers from his pocket.

"Here are your reports, my dear fellow, and very well thumbed, I assure you. I made excellent arrangements, and they are only delayed one day upon their way. I must compliment you exceedingly upon the zeal and the intelligence which you have shown over an extraordinarily difficult case."

I was still rather raw over the deception which had been practised upon me, but the warmth of Holmes's praise drove my anger from my mind. I felt also in my heart that he was right in what he said and that it was really best for our purpose that I should not have known that he was upon the moor.

"That's better," said he, seeing the shadow rise from my face. "And now tell me the result of your visit to Mrs. Laura Lyons -- it was not difficult for me to guess that it was to see her that you had gone, for I am already aware that she is the one person in Coombe Tracey who might be of service to us in the matter. In fact, if you had not gone to-day it is exceedingly probable that I should have gone to-morrow."

The sun had set and dusk was settling over the moor. The air had turned chill and we withdrew into the hut for warmth. There sitting together in the twilight, I told Holmes of my conversation with the lady. So interested was he that I had to repeat some of it twice before he was satisfied.

"This is most important," said he when I had concluded, "It fills up a gap which I had been unable to bridge in this most complex affair. You are aware, perhaps, that a close intimacy exists between this lady and the man Stapleton?"

"I did not know of a close intimacy."

"There can be no doubt about the matter. They meet, they write, there is a complete understanding between them. Now, this puts a very powerful weapon into our hands. If I could only use it to detach his wife "

"His wife?"

"I am giving you some information now, in return for all that you have given me. The lady who has passed here as Miss Stapleton is in reality his wife."

"Good heavens, Holmes! Are you sure of what you say? How could he have permitted Sir Henry to fall in love with her?"

"Sir Henry's falling in love could do no harm to anyone except Sir Henry. He took particular care that Sir Henry did not make love to her, as you have yourself observed. I repeat that the lady is his wife and not his sister."

"But why is this elaborate deception?"

"Because he foresaw that she would be very much more useful to him in the character of a free woman."

All my unspoken instincts, my vague suspicions, suddenly took shape and centred upon the naturalist. In that impassive colourless man, with his straw hat and his butterfly-net, I seemed to see something terrible -- a creature of infinite patience and craft, with a smiling face and a murderous heart.

"It is he, then, who is our enemy -- it is he who dogged us in London?"

"So I read the riddle."

"And the warning -- it must have come from her!"

"Exactly."

The shape of some monstrous villainy, half seen, half guessed, loomed through the darkness which had girt me so long.

"But are you sure of this, Holmes? How do you know that the woman is his wife?"

"Because he so far forgot himself as to tell you a true piece of autobiography upon the occasion when he first met you, and I dare say he has many a time regretted it since. He was once a schoolmaster in the north of England. Now, there is no one more easy to trace than a schoolmaster. There are scholastic agencies by which one may identify any man who has been in the profession. A little investigation showed me that a school had come to grief under atrocious circumstances, and that the man who had owned it -- the name was different -- had disappeared with his wife. The descriptions agreed. When I learnt that the missing man was devoted to entomology, the identification was complete."

The darkness was rising, but much was still hidden by the shadows.

"If this woman is in truth his wife, where does Mrs. Laura Lyons come in?" I asked.

"That is one of the points upon which your own researches have shed a light. Your interview with the lady has cleared the situation very much. I did not know about a projected divorce between herself and her husband. In that case, regarding Stapleton as an unmarried man, she counted no doubt upon becoming his wife."

"And when is she undeceived?"

"Why, then we may find the lady of service. It must be our first duty to see her -- both of us -- to-morrow. Don't you think, Watson, that you are away from your charge rather long? Your place should be at Baskerville Hall."

The last red streaks had faded away in the west and night had settled upon the moor. A few faint stars were gleaming in a violet sky.

"One last question, Holmes," I said as I rose, "Surely there is no need of secrecy between you and me. What is the meaning of it all? What is he after?"

Holmes's voice sank as he answered- 'It is murder, Watson -- refined, cold-blooded, deliberate murder. Do not ask me for particulars. My nets are closing upon him, even as his are upon Sir Henry, and with your help he is already almost at my mercy. There is but one danger which can threaten us. It is that he should strike before we are ready to do so.

"Why should we not arrest him at once?"

"My dear Watson, you were born to be a man of action. Your instinct is always to do something energetic. But supposing, for argument's sake, that we had him arrested to-night, what on earth the better off should we be for that?

We could prove nothing against him. There's the devilish cunning of it! If he were acting through a human agent we could get some evidence, but if we were to drag this great dog to the light of day it would not help us in putting a rope round the neck of its master."

Holmes's voice sank as he answered.

"Surely we have a case."

"Not a shadow of one -- only surmise and conjecture. We should be laughed out of court if we came with such a story and such evidence."

"There is Sir Charles's death."

"Found dead without a mark upon him. You and I know that he died of sheer fright, and we know also what frightened him but how are we to get twelve stolid jurymen to know it? What signs are there of a hound? Where are the marks of its fangs? Of course we know that a hound does not bite a dead body and that Sir Charles was dead before ever the brute overtook him. But we have to prove all this, and we are not in a position to do it."

"Well, then, to-night?"

"We are not much better off to-night. Again, there was no direct connection between the hound and the man's death. We never saw the hound. We heard it, but we could not prove that it was running upon this man's trail. There is a complete absence of motive. No, my dear fellow; we must reconcile ourselves to the fact that we have no case at present, and that it is worth our while to run any risk in order to establish one."

"And how do you propose to do so?"

"I have great hopes of what Mrs. Laura Lyons may do for us when the position of affairs is made clear to her. And I have my own plan as well. Sufficient for to-morrow is the evil thereof; but I hope before the day is past to have the upper hand at last."

I could draw nothing further from him, and he walked, lost in thought, as far as the Baskerville gates.

"Are you coming up?"

"Yes; I see no reason for further concealment. But one

last word, Watson. Say nothing of the hound to Sir Henry. Let him think that Selden's death was as Stapleton would have us believe. He will have a better nerve for the ordeal which he will have to undergo to-morrow, when he is engaged, if I remember your report aright, to dine with these people."

"And so am I."

"Then you must excuse yourself and he must go alone. That will be easily arranged. And now, if we are too late for dinner, I think that we are both ready for our suppers."

❏

Holmes Plans Deceitfully

Sir Henry was more pleased than surprised to see Sherlock Holmes, for he had for some days been expecting that recent events would bring him down from London. He did raise his eyebrows, however, when he found that my friend had neither any luggage nor any explanations for its absence. Between us we soon supplied his wants, and then over a belated supper we explained to the baronet as much of our experience as it seemed desirable that he should know. But first I had the unpleasant duty of breaking the news to Barrymore and his wife. To him it may have been an unmitigated relief, but she wept bitterly in her apron. To all the world he was the man of violence, half animal and half demon; but to her he always remained the little wilful boy of her own girlhood, the child who had clung to her hand. Evil indeed is the man who has not one woman to mourn him.

"I've been moping in the house all day since Watson went off in the morning," said the baronet. "I guess I should have some credit, for I have kept my promise. If I hadn't sworn not to go about alone I might have had a more lively evening, for I had a message from Stapleton asking me over there."

"I have no doubt that you would have had a more lively evening," said Holmes drily. "By the way, I don't suppose you appreciate that we have been mourning over you as having broken your neck?"

Sir Henry opened his eyes. "How was that?"

"This poor wretch was dressed in your clothes. I fear your servant who gave them to him may get into trouble with the police."

"That is unlikely. There was no mark on any of them, as far as I know."

"That's lucky for him -- in fact, it's lucky for all of you, since you are all on the wrong side of the law in this matter. I am not sure that as a conscientious detective my first duty is not to arrest the whole household. Watson's reports are most incriminating documents."

"But how about the case?" asked the baronet, "Have you made anything out of the tangle? I don't know that Watson and I are much the wiser since we came down."

"I think that I shall be in a position to make the situation rather more clear to you before long. It has been an exceedingly difficult and most complicated business. There are several points upon which we still want light -- but it is coming all the same."

"We've had one experience, as Watson has no doubt told you. We heard the hound on the moor, so I can swear that it is not all empty superstition. I had something to do with dogs when I was out West, and I know one when I hear one. If you can muzzle that one and put him on a chain I'll be ready to swear you are the greatest detective of all time."

"I think I will muzzle him and chain him all right if you will give me your help."

"Whatever you tell me to do I will do."

"Very good; and I will ask you also to do it blindly, without always asking the reason."

"Just as you like."

"If you will do this I think the chances are that our little problem will soon be solved. I have no doubt."

He stopped suddenly and stared fixedly up over my head into the air. The lamp beat upon his face, and so intent was it and so still that it might have been that of a clear-cut classical statue, a personification of alertness and expectation.

"What is it?" we both cried.

I could see as he looked down that he was repressing some internal emotion. His features were still composed, but his eyes shone with amused exultation.

"Excuse the admiration of a connoisseur," said he as he waved his hand towards the line of portraits which covered the opposite wall, "Watson won't allow that I know anything of art but that is mere jealousy because our views upon the subject differ. Now, these are a really very fine series of portraits."

"Well, I'm glad to hear you say so," said Sir Henry, glancing with some surprise at my friend, "I don't pretend to know much about these things, and I'd be a better judge of a horse or a steer than of a picture. I didn't know that you found time for such things."

"I know what is good when I see it, and I see it now. That's a Kneller, I'll swear, that lady in the blue silk over yonder, and the stout gentleman with the wig ought to be a Reynolds. They are all family portraits, I presume?"

"Everyone."

"Do you know the names?"

"Barrymore has been coaching me in them, and I think I can say my lessons fairly well."

"Who is the gentleman with the telescope?"

"That is Rear-Admiral Baskerville, who served under Rodney in the West Indies. The man with the blue coat

He stopped suddenly and stared
fixedly up over my head into the air.

and the roll of paper is Sir William Baskerville, who was Chairman of Committees of the House of Commons under Pitt."

"And this Cavalier opposite to me -- the one with the black velvet and the lace?"

"Ah, you have a right to know about him. That is the cause of all the mischief, the wicked Hugo, who started the Hound of the Baskervilles. We're not likely to forget him."

I gazed with interest and some surprise upon the portrait.

"Dear me!" said Holmes, "he seems a quiet, meek-mannered man enough, but I dare say that there was a lurking devil in his eyes. I had pictured him as a more robust and ruffianly person."

"There's no doubt about the authenticity, for the name and the date, 1647, are on the back of the canvas."

Holmes said little more, but the picture of the old roysterer seemed to have a fascination for him, and his eyes were continually fixed upon it during supper. It was not until later, when Sir Henry had gone to his room, that I was able to follow the trend of his thoughts. He led me back into the banqueting-hall, his bedroom candle in his hand, and he held it up against the time-stained portrait on the wall.

"Do you see anything there?"

I looked at the broad plumed hat, the curling love-locks, the white lace collar, and the straight, severe face which was framed between them. It was not a brutal countenance, but it was prim hard, and stern, with a firm-set, thin-lipped mouth, and a coldly intolerant eye.

"Is it like anyone you know?"

"There is something of Sir Henry about the jaw."

"Just a suggestion, perhaps. But wait an instant!" He
stood upon a chair, and, holding up the light in his left
hand, he curved his right arm over the broad hat and
round the long ringlets.

"Good heavens!" I cried in amazement.

The face of Stapleton had sprung out of the canvas.

"Ha, you see it now. My eyes have been trained to
examine faces and not their trimmings. It is the first
quality of a criminal investigator that he should see
through a disguise."

"But this is marvellous. It might be his portrait."

"Yes, it is an interesting instance of a throwback, which
appears to be both physical and spiritual. A study of
family portraits is enough to convert a man to the
doctrine of reincarnation. The fellow is a Baskerville --
that is evident."

"With designs upon the succession."

"Exactly. This chance of the picture has supplied us
with one of our most obvious missing links. We have him,
Watson, we have him, and I dare swear that before to-
morrow night he will be fluttering in our net as helpless
as one of his own butterflies. A pin, a cork, and a card,
and we add him to the Baker Street collection!" He burst
into one of his rare fits of laughter as he turned away from
the picture. I have not heard him laugh often, and it has
always boded ill to somebody.

I was up before time in the morning, but Holmes was
afoot earlier still, for I saw him as I dressed, coming up
the drive.

"Yes, we should have a full day to-day," he remarked,
and he rubbed his hands with the joy of action, "The nets
are all in place, and the drag is about to begin. We'll know
before the day is out whether we have caught our big,

leanjawed pike, or whether he has got through the meshes."

"Have you been on the moor already?"

"I have sent a report from Grimpen to Princetown as to the death of Selden. I think I can promise that none of you will be troubled in the matter. And I have also communicated with my faithful Cartwright, who would certainly have pined away at the door of my hut, as a dog does at his master's grave, if I had not set his mind at rest about my safety."

"What is the next move?"

"To see Sir Henry. Ah, here he is!"

"Good morning, Holmes," said the baronet, "You look like a general who is planning a battle with his chief of the staff."

"That is the exact situation. Watson was asking for orders."

"And so do I."

"Very good. You are engaged, as I understand, to dine with our friends the Stapletons to-night."

"I hope that you will come also. They are very hospitable people, and I am sure that they would be very glad to see you."

"I fear that Watson and I must go to London."

"To London?"

"Yes, I think that we should be more useful there at the present juncture."

The baronet's face perceptibly lengthened.

"I hoped that you were going to see me through this business. The Hall and the moor are not very pleasant places when one is alone."

"My dear fellow, you must trust me implicitly and do exactly what I tell you. You can tell your friends that we should have been happy to have come with you, but that urgent business required us to be in town. We hope very soon to return to Devonshire. Will you remember to give them that message?"

"If you insist upon it."

"There is no alternative, I assure you."

I saw by the baronet's clouded brow that he was deeply hurt by what he regarded as our desertion.

"When do you desire to go?" he asked coldly.

"Immediately after breakfast. We will drive in to Coombe Tracey, but Watson will leave his things as a pledge that he will come back to you. Watson, you will send a note to Stapleton to tell him that you regret that you cannot come."

"I have a good mind to go to London with you," said the baronet, "Why should I stay here alone?"

"Because it is your post of duty. Because you gave me your word that you would do as you were told, and I tell you to stay."

"All right, then, I'll stay."

"One more direction! I wish you to drive to Merripit House Send back your trap, however, and let them know that you intend to walk home."

"To walk across the moor?"

"Yes."

"But that is the very thing which you have so often cautioned me not to do."

"This time you may do it with safety. If I had not every confidence in your nerve and courage I would not suggest it, but it is essential that you should do it."

"Then I will do it."

"And as you value your life do not go across the moor in any direction save along the straight path which leads from Merripit House to the Grimpen Road, and is your natural way home."

"I will do just what you say."

"Very good. I should be glad to get away as soon after breakfast as possible, so as to reach London in the afternoon."

I was much astounded by this programme, though I remembered that Holmes had said to Stapleton on the night before that his visit would terminate next day. It had not crossed my mind however, that he would wish me to go with him, nor could I understand how we could both be absent at a moment which he himself declared to be critical. There was nothing for it, however, but implicit obedience; so we bade good-bye to our rueful friend, and a couple of hours afterwards we were at the station of Coombe Tracey and had dispatched the trap upon its return journey. A small boy was waiting upon the platform.

"Any orders, sir?"

"You will take this train to town, Cartwright. The moment you arrive, you will send a wire to Sir Henry Baskerville, in my name, to say that if he finds the pocketbook which I have dropped he is to send it by registered post to Baker Street."

"Yes, sir."

"And ask at the station office if there is a message for me."

The boy returned with a telegram, which Holmes handed to me. It ran:

Wire received. Coming down with unsigned warrant.
Arrive five-forty.
Lestrade.

"That is in answer to mine of this morning. He is the

I was up before time in the morning,
but Holmes was afoot earlier still.

best of the professionals, I think, and we may need his assistance. Now, Watson, I think that we cannot employ our time better than by calling upon your acquaintance, Mrs. Laura Lyons."

His plan of campaign was beginning to be evident. He would use the baronet in order to convince the Stapletons that we were really gone, while we should actually return at the instant when we were likely to be needed. That telegram from London, if mentioned by Sir Henry to the Stapletons, must remove the last suspicions from their minds. Already I seemed to see our nets drawing closer around that leanjawed pike.

Mrs. Laura Lyons was in her office, and Sherlock Holmes opened his interview with a frankness and directness which considerably amazed her.

"I am investigating the circumstances which attended the death of the late Sir Charles Baskerville," said he, "My friend here, Dr. Watson, has informed me of what you have communicated, and also of what you have withheld in connection with that matter."

"What have I withheld?" she asked defiantly.

"You have confessed that you asked Sir Charles to be at the gate at ten o'clock. We know that that was the place and hour of his death. You have withheld what the connection is between these events."

"There is no connection."

"In that case the coincidence must indeed be an extraordinary one. But I think that we shall succeed in establishing a connection, after all. I wish to be perfectly frank with you, Mrs. Lyons. We regard this case as one of murder, and the evidence may implicate not only your friend Mr. Stapleton but his wife as well."

The lady sprang from her chair.

"His wife!" she cried.

"The fact is no longer a secret. The person who has passed for his sister is really his wife."

Mrs. Lyons had resumed her seat. Her hands were grasping the arms of her chair, and I saw that the pink nails had turned white with the pressure of her grip.

"His wife!" she said again. "His wife! He is not a married man."

Sherlock Holmes shrugged his shoulders.

"Prove it to me! Prove it to me! And if you can do so!" The fierce flash of her eyes said more than any words.

"I have come prepared to do so," said Holmes, drawing several papers from his pocket, "Here is a photograph of the couple taken in York four years ago. It is indorsed 'Mr. and Mrs. Vandeleur,' but you will have no difficulty in recognizing him, and her also, if you know her by sight. Here are three written descriptions by trustworthy witnesses of Mr. and Mrs. Vandeleur, who at that time kept St. Oliver's private school. Read them and see if you can doubt the identity of these people."

She glanced at them, and then looked up at us with the set rigid face of a desperate woman.

Mystery is Solved

Our conversation was hampered by the presence of the driver of the hired wagonette, so that we might be forced to talk of trivial matters when our nerves were tense with emotion and anticipation. It was a relief to me, after that unnatural restraint, when we at last passed Frankland's house and knew that we were drawing near to the Hall and to the scene of action. We did not drive up to the door but got down near the gate of the avenue. The wagonette was paid off and ordered to return to Coombe Tracey forthwith, while we started to walk to Merripit House.

"Are you armed, Lestrade?"

The little detective smiled.

"As long as I have my trousers I have a hip-pocket, and as long as I have my hip-pocket I have something in it."

"Good! My friend and I are also ready for emergencies."

"You're mighty close about this affair, Mr. Holmes. What's the game now?"

"A waiting game."

"My word, it does not seem a very cheerful place," said the detective with a shiver, glancing round him at the gloomy slopes of the hill and at the huge lake of fog which lay over the Grimpen Mire, "I see the lights of a house ahead of us."

I tiptoed down the path and stooped behind the low wall.

"That is Merripit House and the end of our journey. I must request you to walk on tiptoe and not to talk above a whisper."

We moved cautiously along the track as if we were bound for the house, but Holmes halted us when we were about two hundred yards from it.

"This will do," said he. "These rocks upon the right make an admirable screen."

"We are to wait here?"

"Yes, we shall make our little ambush here. Get into this hollow, Lestrade. You have been inside the house, have you not, Watson? Can you tell the position of the rooms? What are those latticed windows at this end?"

"I think they are the kitchen windows."

"And the one beyond, which shines so brightly?"

"That is certainly the dining-room."

"The blinds are up. You know the lie of the land best. Creep forward quietly and see what they are doing -- but for heaven's sake don't let them know that they are watched!"

I tiptoed down the path and stooped behind the low wall which surrounded the stunted orchard. Creeping in its shadow I reached a point whence I could look straight through the uncurtained window.

There were only two men in the room, Sir Henry and Stapleton. They sat with their profiles towards me on either side of the round table. Both of them were smoking cigars, and coffee and wine were in front of them. Stapleton was talking with animation, but the baronet looked pale and distrait. Perhaps the thought of that lonely walk across the ill-omened moor was weighing heavily upon his mind.

As I watched them, Stapleton rose and left the room, while Sir Henry filled his glass again and leaned back in his chair, puffing at his cigar. I heard the creak of a door and the crisp sound of boots upon gravel. The steps passed along the path on the other side of the wall under which I crouched. Looking over, I saw the naturalist pause at the door of an out-house in the corner of the orchard. A key turned in a lock, and as he passed in there was a curious scuffling noise from within. He was only a minute or so inside, and then I heard the key turn once more and he passed me and reentered the house. I saw him rejoin his guest, and I crept quietly back to where my companions were waiting to tell them what I had seen.

"You say, Watson, that the lady is not there?" Holmes asked when I had finished my report.

"No."

"Where can she be, then, since there is no light in any other room except the kitchen?"

"I cannot think where she is."

I have said that over the great Grimpen Mire there hung a dense, white fog. It was drifting slowly in our direction and banked itself up like a wall on that side of us, low but thick and well defined. The moon shone on it, and it looked like a great shimmering ice-field, with the heads of the distant tors as rocks borne upon its surface. Holmes's face was turned towards it, and he muttered impatiently as he watched its sluggish drift.

"It's moving towards us, Watson."

"Is that serious?"

"Very serious, indeed -- the one thing upon earth which could have disarranged my plans. He can't be very long, now. It is already ten o'clock. Our success and even his life may depend upon his coming out before the fog is over the path."

The night was clear and fine above us. The stars shone cold and bright, while a half-moon bathed the whole scene in a soft, uncertain light. Before us lay the dark bulk of the house, its serrated roof and bristling chimneys hard outlined against the silver-spangled sky. Broad bars of golden light from the lower windows stretched across the orchard and the moor. One of them was suddenly shut off. The servants had left the kitchen. There only remained the lamp in the dining-room where the two men, the muderous host and the unconscious guest, still chatted over their cigars.

Every minute that white woolly plain which covered one-half of the moor was drifting closer and closer to the house. Already the first thin wisps of it were curling across the golden square of the lighted window. The farther wall of the orchard was already invisible, and the trees were standing out of a swirl of white vapour. As we watched it, the fog-wreaths came crawling round both corners of the house and rolled slowly into one dense bank on which the upper floor and the roof floated like a strange ship upon a shadowy sea. Holmes struck his hand passionately upon the rock in front of us and stamped his feet in his impatience.

"If he isn't out in a quarter of an hour, the path will be covered. In half an hour, we won't be able to see our hands in front of us."

"Shall we move farther back upon higher ground?"

"Yes, I think it would be as well."

So as the fog-bank flowed onward we fell back before it until we were half a mile from the house, and still that dense white sea, with the moon silvering its upper edge, swept slowly and inexorably on.

"We are going too far," said Holmes, "We dare not take

The Hound of The Baskervilles—7

The night was clear and fine above us.

the chance of his being overtaken before he can reach us. At all costs we must hold our ground where we are." He dropped on his knees and clapped his ear to the ground. "Thank God, I think that I hear him coming."

A sound of quick steps broke the silence of the moor. Crouching among the stones we stared intently at the silver-tipped bank in front of us. The steps grew louder, and through the fog, as through a curtain, there stepped the man whom we were awaiting. He looked round him in surprise as he emerged into the clear, starlit night. Then he came swiftly along the path, passed close to where we lay, and went on up the long slope behind us. As he walked, he glanced continually over either shoulder, like a man who is ill at ease.

"Hist!" cried Holmes, and I heard the sharp click of a cocking pistol. "Look out! It's coming!"

There was a thin, crisp, continuous patter from somewhere in the heart of that crawling bank. The cloud was within fifty yards of where we lay, and we glared at it, all three, uncertain what horror was about to break from the heart of it. I was at Holmes's elbow, and I glanced for an instant at his face. It was pale and exultant, his eyes shining brightly in the moonlight. But suddenly, they started forward in a rigid, fixed stare, and his lips parted in amazement. At the same instant, Lestrade gave a yell of terror and threw himself face downward upon the ground. I sprang to my feet, my inert hand grasping my pistol, my mind paralyzed by the dreadful shape which had sprung out upon us from the shadows of the fog. A hound it was, an enormous coal-black hound, but not such a hound as mortal eyes have ever seen. Fire burst from its open mouth, its eyes glowed with a smouldering glare, its muzzle and hackles and dewlap were outlined in flickering flame. Never in the delirious dream of a disordered brain could anything more savage, more appalling, more hellish be conceived than that dark form and savage face which broke upon us out of the wall of fog.

With long bounds the huge black creatwe was leaping down the track, following hard upon the footsteps of our friend. So paralyzed were we by the apparition that we allowed him to pass before we had recovered our nerve. Then Holmes and I both fired together, and the creature gave a hideous howl, which showed that one at least had hit him. He did not pause, however, but bounded onward. Far away on the path we saw Sir Henry looking back, his face white in the moonlight, his hands raised in horror, glaring helplessly at the frightful thing which was hunting him down.

But that cry of pain from the hound had blown all our fears to the winds. If he was vulnerable he was mortal, and if we could wound him we could kill him. Never have I seen a man run as Holmes ran that night. I am reckoned fleet of foot, but he outpaced me as much as I outpaced the little professional. In front of us as we flew up the track we heard scream after scream from Sir Henry and the deep roar of the hound. I was in time to see the beast spring upon its victim, hurl him to the ground, and worry at his throat. But the next instant Holmes had emptied five barrels of his revolver into the creature's flank. With a last howl of agony and a vicious snap in the air, it rolled upon its back, four feet pawing furiously, and then fell limp upon its side. I stooped, panting, and pressed my pistol to the dreadful, shimmering head, but it was useless to press the trigger. The giant hound was dead.

Sir Henry lay insensible where he had fallen. We tore away his collar, and Holmes breathed a prayer of gratitude when we saw. that there was no sign of a wound and that the rescue had been in time. Already our friend's eyelids shivered and he made a feeble effort to move. Lestrade thrust his brandy-flask between the baronet's teeth, and two frightened eyes were looking up at us.

"My God!" he whispered. "What was it? What, in heaven's name, was it?"

"It's dead, whatever it is," said Holmes, "We've laid the family ghost once and for ever."

In mere size and strength it was a terrible creature which was lying stretched before us. It was not a pure bloodhound and it was not a pure mastiff; but it appeared to be a combination of the two -- gaunt, savage, and as large as a small lioness.

Questions Based on the Story

Chapter–1
Dr. James Mortimer with Sherlock Holmes

Q. 1 Why had Dr. James Mortimer come over to Sherlock's house?

Q. 2 What does C.C.H. mean, according to Sherlock Holmes?

Chapter–2
Footprints of Hound

Q. 1 What was the habit of Sir Charles Baskerville before going to bed at night?

Q. 2 Whose footprints had Dr. Mortimer seen?

Chapter–3
Holmes Interrogates Sir Henry Baskerville

Q. 1 Who was Henry Baskerville?

Q. 2 What did Henry Baskerville tell Sherlock about his new pair of boots?

Chapter–4
Holmes Threads the Events

Q. 1 Who was Barrymore?

Q. 2 Why did Sherlock want Dr. Watson to visit Baskerville Hall?

Dr. Watson Visits Baskerville Hall

Q. 1 Who along with Dr. Watson went to Baskerville Hall ?

Q. 2 Who pointed with his whip that they had reached Baskerville Hall?

Reports of Dr. Watson

Q. 1 What did Dr. Watson tell Sherlock about Sir Henry Baskerville in his first report?

Q. 2 Who was the beautiful neighbour of Dr. Watson in Baskerville Hall?

Chapter–7

Watson Establishes Two Important Facts

Q. 1 What two important facts had Dr. Watson established during his stay at Baskerville Hall?

Q. 2 Who had made Stapleton his almoner upon several occasions ?

Holmes Joins Watson

Q. 1 Whose well-known voice had Dr. Watson heard?

Q. 2 Who was Mrs. Laura Lyons?

Holmes Plans Deceitfully

Q. 1 Who was William Baskerville?

Q. 2 What was written in the telegram which Holmes handed over to Dr. Watson?

Mystery is Solved

Q. 1   Why did Sherlock halt others from approaching the house?

Q. 2   Who was the real culprit responsible for the murder of Sir Charles Baskerville?

www.ingramcontent.com/pod-product-compliance
Lightning Source LLC
LaVergne TN
LVHW020052210726
843507LV00015B/1800